Be sure to look for all the great McGee and Me! books and videos at your favorite bookstore.

Focus on the Family®
PRESENTS

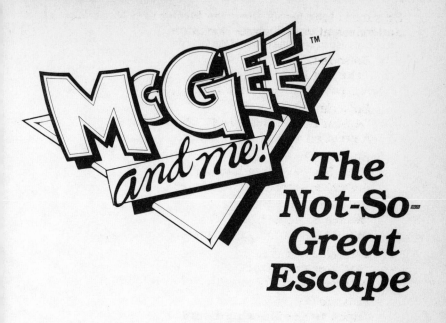

McGEE™ and me!

The Not-So- Great Escape

Bill Myers and Ken C. Johnson

Tyndale House Publishers, Inc.
Wheaton, Illinois

For Mike, Steve, Rob, and George—
men committed to using the power of film for good.

Front cover illustration copyright © 1989 by Morgan Weistling
Interior illustrations by Nathan Greene, copyright © 1989
by Tyndale House Publishers, Inc.

Library of Congress Catalog Card Number 89-51394
ISBN 0-8423-4167-6
McGee and Me!, McGee, and *McGee and Me!* logo
are trademarks of Living Bibles International
Copyright © 1989 by Living Bibles International
Printed in the United States of America

00 99 98 97
11 10 9 8

Contents

"Fix your thoughts on what is true and good and right. Think about things that are pure and lovely, and dwell on the fine, good things in others" (Philippians 4:8, *The Living Bible*).

ONE
The Space Creeper Strikes Again

Thirty-two right, fourteen left, seventeen right, and finally nothing left . . . to do but wait, that is. Then slowly the lock on the door of my lunar prison cell began to open. I stood there, gripped with suspense. The hefty door swung wide, revealing what I'd worked on for these many months—my freedom. Though it had taken only a few moments and some brain bending calculations to program the lunar lock and figure out its combination, it had seemed like days. OK, so it had been days: 136 days to be exact. But, hey, who's counting? I never really was that good in math anyway.

I was counting on one thing, though: Getting out of there! There had never been a prison in the star system that could hold the sinister Space Villain for long. Besides, I needed a change of scenery. Between choking down the galactic glob they call food and playing several games of "stare down" with the four walls, this hadn't exactly been a summer vacation. So, with a song in my heart and a sneer on my lips, off I went.

I snaked my way swiftly and quietly down corridor after darkened corridor. A thousand thoughts raced through my head: Had I tripped the alarm? Were the android guards on to me yet? Was my hidden space pod still intact and waiting for me in Quadrant Three? Is Colonel Crater's Fried Chicken open this time of night?

Suddenly a phaser blast pierced the darkness. It ricocheted right in front of my feet. As I frantically dodged the blast I realized one of my questions had been answered: the guards were definitely on to me.

I moved down the corridor, slipping through one hallway and down the other with moves that would make Michael Jackson turn green with nausea . . . uh, envy. The android guards were hot on my trail—this little game of blast attack was getting old fast. If I could just think of something to throw them off track. Maybe get the goons to sit down and swap nut-and-bolt recipes or something. Unfortunately, I had left my Betty Cosmos Cookbook back in my cell. So instead I chose to stick to my original brilliant plan: Run!

Another series of laser bursts grazed past my heels and exploded in front of me. The shots tore a hole in the air vent beside me. Aha! I thought. Their brainless blasting has created an escape route. Amidst a blaze of laserfire I dove for the air duct and squeezed inside. It was just big enough for a notorious space villain of my size.

As I scooted down the shaft I let out a hideous cry to taunt the trigger-happy space 'droids. "Booooo-ah-

ah-ah-ahhh. No one can stop the dastardly Villain, mad master of interplanetary bad guys. No one. Boo-ah-ah-ah!" My eerie laughter echoed down the air shafts, sending chills up the spine of every space guard in the quadrant. (A pretty neat trick considering the guards were all androids—you know, fancy robots.)

As I worked my way down the air shafts toward my hidden space pod, I recalled how I had gotten into this fix in the first place. I'd been busy doing my usual cosmic crime stuff throughout fourteen star systems (talk about overworked!): hijacking Diamel freighters the planet Zirconia, pillaging spice mines on planet Paprika, stealing the sacred singing stones of Jagger Moon . . . not returning an overdue book from the public library in Cleveland. Yes, I was an interplanetary pirate without equal (and without brains, according to the space cops who'd found my prints all over everything).

Finally the Galactic Governing Council sent out an elite group of crime fighters, The Blue Fox Squadron. Their leader was my old rival, Cyborg II. There was even a bounty of 2 million greckles for my capture (about eight bucks in real money). However, for a goody two-shoes like Cyborg II, the reward didn't matter. No, not to Mr. Good Guy . . . Mr. Straight and Narrow . . . Mr. Mom and Asteroid Pie. He did good deeds just for the sake of doing good deeds—things like helping little old ladies cross the Forbidden Zone. So it was no surprise that he would pursue my highly dangerous self across the universe, risking life and limb for peanuts (unsalted, of course). After all, he was the

11

hero. It was his job to do that kind of thing.

My job was to be an evil space villain. Some job. I mean, the pay and hours were lousy. I was chased night and day, often had to go without sleep, and usually ran dangerously low on fuel (and Twinkies). And nobody ever sent me birthday presents . . . believe me, being a fugitive is a real pain.

Well, one night I fell right into one of Cyborg's clever little traps. I'd stopped at a safety inspection station—you know, where they check for faulty thermal reactors, hydro-converters, and any illegal fruit being taken across the border. When I eased into the station, a trooper approached my craft. He asked for my travel code, flight papers, and if I was carrying any melons or mangoes. When I handed him my papers, he lifted his visor and looked at me with a steely-eyed stare I knew all too well. It was Cyborg II! Faster than you can say, "Obee Won, Kenobee," the rest of the Blue Fox Squadron sur-rounded my ship. Their eyes—and their blasters—were aimed right at me.

There I was, surrounded by fifty of the best crime fighters in the galaxy. Now what? I thought. Should I fight to the finish? Create a smoke screen? Try to talk my way out of it?

Then it came to me; it was perhaps the most bril-liant scheme I had ever conceived! I slowly lifted my arms into the air. Then through sneering lips I whispered those magic words: "I give up."

You know, sometimes I'm so clever I scare myself.

Next thing I knew I was hauled into space court, yelled at by the space judge, fined seventy-five greckles for the case of melons they found hidden in my trunk, and sentenced to eternity in the Mugsy Moon Rock Institute for the Criminally Clumsy. I'd been there ever since.

Until now, that is. Now I was making my escape. And things were going just as I'd expected them to—rotten.

I ended up crawling around in the stupid air shaft for about an hour trying to find Quadrant Three where I'd hidden my faithful space pod. No luck. It was still hidden. Then I noticed a flashing light through the grill of a vent up ahead. "Aha! Now we're getting somewhere," I exclaimed.

Drawing closer, I heard the squawk of a guard 'droid's two-way radio. I anxiously peered out and saw the mechanical moron pacing back and forth. He obviously had his sensors on the lookout for you-know-who.

Suddenly his radio came alive with an urgent transmission: "This is Blue Fox Leader. Any sign of escaped villain in Quadrant Five?"

"Negative, Blue Fox," the guard responded. "All quiet here."

"Be on your toes," Blue Fox said. "This villain's a sneaky little character."

"Affirmative, Blue Fox. I've got my eyes peeled and my nose to the ground. Over and out."

Well, that sounded painful, even for an android. But it was also enlightening. Not only was every guard in the compound hot on my trail, but Cyborg II and his Blue Fox boys were close. Real close. That thought put a knot in my stomach the size of Jupiter. One thing was sure; I didn't spell relief "C-Y-B-O-R-G."

Well, if I was in Quadrant Five, then Quadrant Three was nearby. (I'm just great with numbers like that.) However, with a maze of air shafts leading a thousand different directions, Quadrant Three wasn't going to be easy to find. There was one thing that would make that search a little easier, though: the guard's radio. I could use it to pick up on the good guys' chit-chat and maybe avoid an unpleasant encounter or two. Besides, if things got really boring, maybe I could tune in on the Cubs' game.

Great. Now for the hard part—getting the radio away from this bucket of bolts. With my luck, it was probably a Christmas present, and he was going to be all sentimental about it and wanna keep it. Of course, I needed it more than he did. I just had to convince him of that. Right. Unfortunately, he was bigger than me. In fact, he was the biggest android I'd ever seen. He made Hulk Hogan look like Pee Wee Herman. I, on the other hand, make Pee Wee Herman look like King Kong. . . . I think you get the picture.

But I put all my brain power into action and came up with a plan. I'd wait for the 'droid to pass underneath me, crown him on the noggin' with the air vent grill, then jump down, scoop up his radio and immobilizer-blaster, and be merrily on my way.

The plan worked great . . . well, except for a few slight catches. Slight catch number one: my finger. I got it caught in the grill. Since the grill weighed as much as yours truly, you can imagine what happened next. We both came crashing down on top of the guard, knocking the mechanical wonder to the floor.

Then came slight catch number two.

The blow knocked the 'droid down. What it didn't do was knock him out. I'd forgotten one little thing— 'droids are machines—you can't knock a machine out. Soooo, it was like hitting a grizzly bear with a house shoe—the only thing that gets knocked out is your teeth. As he slowly got up, I knew this could mean some heavy hand-to-hand combat. You know, kung-fu, karate, chop suey.

I decided to take the simplest route. I ran between his legs. I must have really confused his circuits because he started spinning around, trying to see where I'd gone. Every time he turned to find me, I'd run back between his legs. Pretty soon the wires in the 'droid's neck got wound so tight they snapped. I heard this pop and zing, and he conveniently sank to the ground, a pile of limp metal and fizzling wires.

Ha! And they think I'm brainless.

I scooped up his radio and immobilizer and bounded toward the vent. I chuckled as I crawled up and out of sight. "Assignment Radio Raid" had gone off after all. OK, so it wasn't exactly what you might call a textbook ambush Rambo-style, but it got the job done.

As I continued to trek through the endless air shafts, I occasionally picked up discussions between troopers in certain Quadrant numbers. I was getting closer to finding my space pod—but the radio transmissions showed that Cyborg II was getting closer to finding me, too.

I came to another vent and peered out. There were familiar markings on the wall: Q4S7—Quadrant Four,

Sector Seven. All right! One Quadrant away. Soon I'd be neatly tucked into my space pod and blasting off to freedom. "Colonel Crater's Fried Chicken, here I come!"

Suddenly, a familiar voice came blasting across the radio: "Cyborg II, this is Blue Fox Leader. Quadrant Four, Sector Seven is secure. Do you copy?"

Yipes! He was right on top of me!

"Roger, Blue Fox. No sign of Creeper yet," Cyborg II answered.

Just then I heard the haunting sound of footsteps echoing through the corridor below. "Keep your eyes peeled, Cyborg II," I heard someone exclaim.

I peeked through the vent and sure enough, there he was, a guard 'droid in tow, drawing closer with every step. My fear suddenly vanished. Why should I be afraid? This was perfect. He didn't know I was up here. For once I was the hammer, he was the nail. I was the cat, he was the mouse. I was the little kid, he was the sucker . . . well, you know what I mean.

Lifting the immobilizer, I drew a bead on the 'droid. I'd nail him first, then Cyborg II. Oh, I'd just wing them. You know, put them out of commission long enough for me escape. I mean, even we wicked space villains have a little heart.

Cyborg II continued waltzing toward me, unaware of my presence. His crazy 'droid followed him, glancing around and whistling some old tune. I think it was the theme song from "The Jetsons." They were getting closer, closer. Cyborg II was in range now. I placed my finger on the trigger and slowly, ever so slowly began to squeeze. . . .

Nuts—the rotten guard 'droid was beginning to sing the lyrics now. I wondered if the immobilizer had a setting for "barbecue." I pulled the trigger back. Click . . . Click . . . Fiz . . . Schweeze . . . Rats! The blaster was out of blast. As Cyborg II and the 'droid casually strolled on past, I kept squeezing the trigger, hoping for the best. If that bucket of bolts sang much longer, it might kill me. The faulty phaser just fizzed.

"Darned no-account, two-bit blaster," I hissed. I tossed it in disgust as the off-key, metalic rendition of "The Jetsons" trailed off in the distance.

I sat there pondering my next move. Then another radio transmission broke the silence: "Blue Fox Leader, this is Cyborg II. Do you copy?"

"Go ahead, Cyborg II, I copy."

"Sir, we've discovered a small space craft in Quadrant Three, Sector Twelve. I think you ought to check it out."

"On my way, Cyborg II. Over and out."

Well, if that wouldn't fry the hair off a wookie. Now, they'd found my space pod. The one I worked on in space prison metal shop for months. (I told the guards I was building a flying toaster.) The one I'd hidden away so carefully so I could use it to escape. Oh well, I really didn't want to escape anyway. I was beginning to like it here. Pleasant surroundings. Courteous staff. Fine dining. Yeah, right.

I made a mad dash down the air shaft (as mad a dash as you can make crawling on bony knees). I crawled so fast, I wore holes in the knees of my prison fatigues. Hey, at least I was in style now.

I hoped to reach my space pod in time to spoil Blue Fox's party. I reached the air vent in Quadrant Three and hesitantly took a peek below. I was too late.

Cyborg II was milling about my beloved pod as another Blue Fox trooper came up.

"What is it?" the trooper asked.

"The Creeper's space pod. Set your immobilizers on 'massacre'! We'll destroy this thing before he can put it to use!"

Phasers on "massacre," *I thought.* Gee, I guess they're not kidding around. *My only hope was that the pod, made of pure titanium steel, would withstand the phaser blast. If it didn't, I was going to need a lot of duct tape and crazy glue.*

The Blue Fox boys began an all-out assault on my tiny space craft. I had to admit I was pleased to see they weren't doing much damage. Their phaser blasts bounced off like tennis balls. Then, just as I decided my ship was going to survive, Cyborg II threw down his blaster in frustration and gave the pod a good swift kick.

BONK! The little space craft shattered into a million useless little pieces.

"Drat. Lousy, two-bit, no-account titanium," I hissed. *Oh, sure, the stuff can withstand a fifty megaton explosion. But give it a little punt, and "crunch," it goes all to pieces on you.*

Well, I was done for. Clobbered! Slaughtered! Trashed! Kicked! Whipped! Annihilated! Hammered! You get the idea. It didn't matter, though. After all, it was all just in fun.

Oh, didn't I tell you? This whole galactic battle was just imagination. Yup. In fact, the whole thing had taken place in my little buddy Nick's front yard, not in the far reaches of outer space.

As for my titanium-covered space pod, well, I guess you could say it was actually a pigskin-covered football. The proton blasters? Harmless little toy guns. The maze of air shafts I've been crawling through . . . well, that was simply the old drain gutter that goes down the side of the house. Even the victorious Cyborg II and Blue Fox boys were none other than Nick and his pal, Louis.

Get the picture?

Now before you get all excited and upset, think it over. A make-believe mission is much better than a real one. No one ever gets hurt, and the clean-up expenses after a battle are almost nil. In fact, there is really only one drawback . . . getting stuck playing the villain. I mean, basically the villain is a real loser. That's OK, though. Who wants the bad guys to win anyway? Besides, if you play your cards right, even the villain can have a small victory once in a while.

Like thinking up a neat little trick to end the game in your favor.

"A valiant effort, earthling," I said to Nick via the walkie-talkie. "But that was only a three-dimensional projection of my pod."

"McGee, that's not fair!" Nicholas shouted. "We creamed you!"

Nick was right . . . but since when do wicked space villains ever play fair?

"Until we meet again," I called. Then I gave him one final laugh. The famous "World's-Most-Wicked-Space-Villain" cackle: "Booo-ah-ah-ah-ahhhh!"

TWO
Night of the Blood Freaks

"Cheater!" Nicholas shouted into his walkie-talkie.

He hated it when McGee did that. Any time Nick was about to get the upper hand in one of their imaginary games, McGee would suddenly change the rules. Nicholas knew he and Louis had captured the Creeper's space pod fair and square. They'd won! But nooooo. Suddenly the space pod was just a 3-D picture, and Mr. Creeper McGee had disappeared.

It happened all the time, and it always made Nick furious. Oh well, that was one of the things you had to put up with when a cartoon drawing was your best friend.

Nick and Louis stood over the somewhat flattened football. It had served well as the Creeper's space pod. Now, thanks to their limitless imaginations, it would become something else. Maybe an alien egg about to hatch little alienettes, or a space slug about to spew space slime or . . . or . . .

"Nicholas, come on in. It'll be getting dark

soon." It was Mom, calling from the front porch.

Nicholas frowned. Moms never understood intergalactic warfare. You could be defending the freedom of the entire galaxy . . . but if it was lunchtime, forget it. Mutant invaders could be threatening our gene pools . . . but if you forgot to put on your coat before going out, too bad. And if you had any homework? Well, you could kiss any superhero activity good-bye. After all, what was more important? Getting an *A* on a spelling quiz or saving all humanoid life-forms as we know them?

"Oh, Mom . . . ," Nicholas protested.

"Come in—now!"

Suddenly the galaxy's safety didn't seem quite so important. Maybe it was the way she said, "Now!" In any case, Nick knew she meant business. So with a heavy sigh he started toward the porch.

"Getting dark soon?" Louis taunted with a smirk at Nicholas. He loved to tease Nick about his parents. They seemed to have all sorts of rules Nick had to follow—what he could do, what he couldn't do, what music he could listen to, how many hours of TV he could watch. In short, if it was fun, Louis figured Nick's folks had a rule against it.

The boys raced up the stairs and threw open the door to Nicholas's room.

"I don't know, Nick," Louis said with a laugh as he plopped down on the bed. "On TV, Cyborg's mom always makes him come in when it gets dark."

Nick spun around and fired off a good burst of imaginary neutrons from his proton blaster. Fortunately it was still set on "massacre." Louis grabbed his chest and did one of his better dying routines. It was beautiful. He choked, he gasped, he sputtered. Then, just when you thought it was all over, he gave one last twitch. Nick had to grin. It was a brilliant performance. On a scale of one to ten, this was definitely an eleven.

Laughing, Nick took off his helmet and Louis reached for the newspaper they'd brought from downstairs.

"Hey, check it out," Louis said as he turned to the movie section. *"Night of the Blood Freaks, Part IV* starts tomorrow. And it's in 3-D."

"No kidding?" Nicholas asked. He crossed over to the bed for a better look.

"Remember last year," Louis asked, "in *Twilight of the Blood Freaks,* when he got those guys at the campfire?"

"Uh, no," Nicholas said, clearing his throat slightly. "I didn't see it. My folks wouldn't let me."

"Man, they don't let you do anything."

"Hey, that was a year ago," Nick protested. "I'm a lot older now, all right?"

Louis gave a shrug and looked back to the ad in the paper. It was as gory as the title. "Have you seen the commercial?" he asked.

Actually, Nick couldn't have helped but see the commercial. It had been running on TV for the last couple of days. It was really gross and really stupid . . . which probably meant the film would be a smash.

"Yeah, I've seen it," Nick said.

The two boys looked at each other. Each knew exactly what the other was thinking. (That was one of the neat things about having a close friend.) Slowly, they each took a breath and started speaking, together, "First there was *Dawn of the Blood Freaks* . . ."

They made their voices as deep and ominous as they could. Slowly they rose from the bed and sat on its edge. Their volume began to grow. "Then . . . *Day of the Blood Freaks.*"

They continued, sounding louder and scarier with each word. "Then . . . *Twilight of the Blood Freaks.*"

They plopped their feet down hard on the floor at exactly the same time. "But now . . ." Slowly they rose to their feet. "As shadows begin to fall it's . . . *Night of the Blood Freaks!*"

They screamed and groaned at the top of their lungs, their bodies bouncing and jerking out of control. One minute it looked like they were doing Frankenstein. The next, some new dance step. Then they grabbed their throats and began to cough and choke—all the time screaming their lungs out.

Meanwhile, several families on both sides of the Martins' home stopped what they were doing. What was that sound? What was going on? A few even stepped out onto their front porch for a better listen. From all the screaming and shouting, it was pretty obvious that someone was either being tortured or murdered. Maybe both.

But a few neighbors didn't pay any attention to the racket. They knew Nicholas. They knew about his imagination.

When Nicholas and his family had first moved into Grandma's house, they were pretty excited. After all, here was a fantastic Victorian house that was over a hundred years old. Who knew what secrets the attic held? Who knew what was under those creaky floorboards in the hallway? Who knew which loose bricks in the basement could be moved to discover a secret passageway?

These were the things they expected. What they didn't expect were drafty rooms in the winter or cold showers in the morning (whenever the hot water heater was on the fritz—which was a lot). Above all, they certainly didn't expect a house without a dishwasher! I mean, this was nearly the twenty-first century, for crying out loud. Surely Grandma would have a dishwasher!

Well, to be honest, Grandma did have a dishwasher. But like everything else in the house it was a "teensy bit on the broken side." And since Dad wasn't famous for being a handyman (well, he was famous—but in the wrong way), they had to wait and bring in a repairman.

Until then, guess whose children got to wash and dry the dishes by hand? Tonight it was Sarah's turn to wash and Nicholas's turn to dry. They'd had fried chicken with mashed potatoes and gravy. Grandma's favorite. But not Sarah's. It's not that she minded the taste. It was the cleaning up she hated. Especially the gravy. Especially after they let it set around for half an hour and it had dried into rubbery, crusty gunk. And, as we all know, once gunk dries, it's impossible to scrape off of dishes. Sarah tried—but not without plenty of sighs, whines, and sarcastic comments done as only a girl going on fourteen can do them.

"This is gross," she muttered. "Why do I always get stuck washing on the gunk days?"

She opened the lid to the plastic garbage can and began to chisel at the next plate. Chicken bones, gravy, and a few hidden green beans bounced and splattered against an empty milk carton.

Whatever, the family dog, was right there, too. Actually, Whatever was mostly Sarah's dog. Nicholas didn't care much for the little fur ball. The critter always seemed to be whining and yapping. Come to think of it, maybe that was why Sarah and Whatever were such good pals—they were so much alike.

Anyway, Whatever was standing off to the side barking and begging. He always did that when they had chicken. Forget the stewed tomatoes, the liver, the cooked cauliflower. Anytime you'd try to slip a handful of those delicacies under the table to him so your plate looked clean, he was nowhere to be found. Come chicken night, though, you couldn't get rid of the pest.

"Make sure he doesn't get any of those bones," Mom warned Sarah as she headed into the family room.

Sarah sighed—her answer to just about everything these days. She knew Whatever liked to chew the bones. She also knew that chicken bones cracked and splintered, and that if Whatever got any and swallowed them, he might really hurt himself.

She knew all this—but she also knew how much he liked chicken.

At first she was able to ignore him—but the persistent little critter kept sitting there whining and begging with the most pitiful look on his face. Of course, Nicholas thought he always looked pitiful. But this time, he was pitifully pitiful.

The dog kept working on Sarah's emotions. He used every trick in the begging handbook. Droopy eyes. Pathetic whines. Sad sighs. Nick thought it was disgusting. Revolting. The fact that it was exactly what he used to do to get his way with his parents never even dawned on him.

Finally, it worked. Sarah gave in.

It wasn't a big piece. Just a chicken wing. And she really didn't "officially" give it to Whatever. She just sort of let it fall on the floor. Then, before she could grab it, he sort of took it and ran off.

Nicholas started to say something (loud enough, of course, for Mom to hear). Then Sarah shot him the old "If-you-know-what's-good-for-you-you'll-keep-your-mouth-shut" look. Normally that look would be just what Nick needed to make him say something. But having battled the Space Creeper all afternoon, Nick wasn't ready for another fight.

Instead he asked quietly, under his breath, "You sure you want him eating that?"

"Don't sweat it; he loves chicken," she muttered. "One piece isn't going to hurt him. No biggie."

But for Whatever, it was about to become a biggie. A life and death biggie . . .

THREE
Grounded

The next morning, *Night of the Blood Freaks* was the talk of the school.

They talked about it on the bus. They talked about it at recess. They talked about it at lunch. The lunch talks were the best. Usually, one of the guys would go into great gory details over what he expected to see. And usually one of the girls would look down at the ketchup dripping off her hamburger . . . and suddenly lose her appetite.

Later in the day, the kids started drawing pictures and passing them around. Dripping fangs here. Crazed, bloodshot eyes there. Of course, Nick drew the best. That was one thing he could do . . . draw. He'd never been too much into drawing gore. But after a few tries he was able to get the hang of it. Pretty soon his stuff was as bad as everyone else's.

Even then, though, even as he was drawing the snarling faces and chewed up victims, a part of him felt kind of uneasy. He wasn't sure how or why . . . but somehow, some way, a part of him knew it was wrong.

It wasn't a big feeling. No shouting voices, no flashing neon signs. Instead, it was kind of a quiet, almost queasy feeling. Some people would call it his conscience. Nick and his folks would say it was God. In any case, if Nick wanted to, he could ignore that feeling. He could let all the excitement and good times drown it out. . . .

And, since that's what he wanted, that's what he did. The uneasy feeling disappeared almost as quickly as it had come. He'd pay attention to it some other time. Right now, he was going to go along with the gang. Just now, he'd let them slap him on the back and tell him how good his gore was.

On the way home everyone was still talking about the film—especially Louis. "The soundtrack to the movie is by Death Threat!" he exclaimed.

The kids on the bus all nodded in approval. Renee, not to be outdone, threw in her two-cents worth. "I've seen all the Freak movies," she bragged.

"Seen them?" Louis chirped. "You starred in them!"

Everyone laughed. They usually did whenever Louis zinged someone. Renee gave him the usual roll of her eyes. Still, she had to admit he was pretty sharp.

Finally, the bus pulled to a stop and the doors hissed open.

"So what do you think?" Louis asked Nicholas

as they headed for the door. "Can you make it to the 2:15 matinee tomorrow?"

"It'll be great!" Nicholas exclaimed as they stepped into the bright sunlight.

But Louis couldn't let it go. Here was another chance to razz Nick about his folks. So, of course, being the good friend he was, Louis did just that.

"Think your mom and dad will let you out of the house?" By the twinkle in Louis's eyes Nicholas knew he was only kidding.

Still, Nick had a reputation to keep up. He didn't want Louis to think he was some wimp who always had to check with his folks for permission. So Nicholas took a chance. Or, rather, he took a guess. . . .

"Hey, I can handle my folks. No sweat."

"All right!" Louis high-fived Nick and they headed for their homes.

When Nick threw open the back door to his house everyone was in a panic. Sarah was running around looking for an empty box. Mom was shouting orders from the hallway. Little sister Jamie sat on the kitchen stool looking very frightened.

"What happened? What's wrong?" Nicholas asked with concern.

Jamie looked at him. She tried to speak, but she could only get out a loud sniff.

"Mom!" Sarah shouted from the basement. "We've got this old apple crate. Will that do?"

"That's fine!" Mom called. "Grab a beach towel and put it in the bottom so he'll be comfortable."

"What's going on?" Nicholas asked louder.

Suddenly Mom came bursting into the room. In her arms was Whatever. But instead of being his usual cheery, obnoxious self, he lay very still and very quiet. Only an occasional whimper escaped him.

"It's Whatever," Mom explained. "There's something wrong with his stomach."

"Oh, Mom . . . ," Jamie started to cry.

"It's OK, Pumpkin. The vet will be able to do something, I'm sure of it." Mom tried her best to stay cool and calm. Jamie tried her best to believe her. Even so, the way Mom raced around the kitchen it was obvious she was pretty concerned.

"Honey," she turned to Nicholas. "Will you get the door for me?"

"Sure, Mom." He crossed to the door and opened it. "What happened?"

"Sarah!" Mom called.

"Coming!" Sarah's voice was closer as she raced up the stairs.

"I don't know," Mom said in answer to Nick's question. "Maybe he got into some poison. Maybe it's something he ate. I don't know."

Just then Sarah appeared from the stairs with the apple crate and a beach towel. By the look on her face it was pretty obvious she knew what had happened—and by the look she shot Nicholas it was pretty obvious she knew he knew. . . .

The chicken bone.

Jamie was crying louder now. She was trying her best not to. For a seven-year-old she was doing a pretty good job. Still, she was only seven . . . and seven meant tears.

"Oh, Pumpkin, he'll be OK," Mom said, then she turned to Sarah. "Fold the towel and set it inside."

Sarah obeyed, then Mom gently lifted Whatever and carefully set him in the box.

"There you go, boy," she said.

The dog looked up and gave a pitiful little whimper. He looked awful.

Sarah's eyes were starting to burn. She bit her lip to hold back her tears.

"Nicholas," Mom said, "Dad should be home any minute. Watch Jamie for me till he gets here."

"Sure."

She gave him a weak little smile as she passed on her way out the door. "Sarah, are you coming?"

Sarah was right behind her. She didn't say a word. She wouldn't even look at Nick. She just stared at the ground and headed out the door.

Nicholas watched silently as they climbed into the car with Whatever and pulled away.

Sarah's voice was crystal clear in his memory: "Don't sweat it; he loves chicken. One piece isn't going to hurt him."

After X-raying Whatever, the veterinarian knew the dog had swallowed something. Probably a bone. The doctor wasn't sure whether she'd have to operate or not. Either way, Whatever would have to spend the night.

On the way home in the car Sarah finally admitted what she had done. "He loves chicken so much," she blurted. "I just couldn't say no."

Mom tried her best to understand, but she was pretty upset. So was Dad when they got home and told him what had happened. How could Sarah be so irresponsible? Didn't she know what the chicken bones would do?

Sarah did know, and she was more than a little sorry. In fact, she was feeling so bad that Mom and Dad decided to go easy on her.

By the time they'd finished dinner, things had cooled down quite a bit. Enough, Nicholas had hoped, that he could ask about seeing the movie. The timing couldn't have been better. Sarah was over at the table doing her homework. Mom was in the kitchen finishing cleaning up. Most important, Dad was upstairs. That was the perfect part! That meant Mom was separated from him . . . alone . . . vulnerable. When the two of them were together, she was always the softer touch. When she was by herself, well, it would be a piece of cake.

Nick started off by playing it cool and nonchalant, like it was nothing. *With any luck,* he thought, *she'll say yes right off the bat.* But this wasn't Nick's lucky day.

"Absolutely not!" she snapped.

The words fell like a death sentence on his ears. "But Mom . . . "

"Why would you want to go see a gross movie like that anyway?"

"'Cause *he's* gross," Sarah shot back from the table. Now it's true that Sarah was feeling pretty bad about her dog. She was feeling pretty crummy about what she had done. But, hey, she was his older sister. She couldn't let a good put-down like that get by her. After all, she did have a reputation to keep up.

"It's not that bad," Nicholas complained to his Mom. But her look made it pretty clear that she'd also seen those TV commercials.

So much for that argument. Nick's brain raced until he found another tactic. It wasn't great and it wasn't very original—but it was all he had, so he used it: "Besides," he stuttered, "everybody's seeing it."

Immediately he could have kicked himself. How could he be so stupid? He'd left himself wide open for the standard parental comeback. Any second those awful, dreaded words would be rolling from his mom's lips: "Oh? You mean if everybody jumped off a cliff, you would jump, too?"

He had to act and act fast. He'd jump in before she had a chance to use that deadly phrase. He would jump in with his final—and his best—line of attack. He would use all of his cunning, his wisdom, his brilliance.

He would beg.

"Come on, Mom . . . Pleeease . . . "

He gave her his best wide-eyed, puppy dog look. It was working. He could see she was starting to soften . . . to break. He had her! Now he'd go in for the kill! Now he'd finish her off with—

"Please what?" a voice asked from the kitchen doorway.

Oh no! It was Dad! Where'd he come from? No fair! Foul! Foul! But it was too late. He had come in to grab a soda from the refrigerator, and his timing couldn't have been worse.

"Nicholas wants to go see a movie with Louis," Mom said.

"Sure, why not?" Dad asked as he poked his head in the fridge.

Nick held his breath. This was it. It could go either way. If Dad just didn't ask the other question—the one that always came up when they talked about movies. If he just didn't ask . . .

"What's it rated?" Aargh! He asked it! That was it. Nick was dead. He knew it.

But instead of an answer, everything was silent. Could it be? Could it be that nobody was going to tell? If no one answered, maybe the question would go away. Chances were good . . . Dad was busy looking for his diet cream soda . . . maybe he wouldn't notice he hadn't gotten an answer. If everybody stayed quiet, then maybe, just maybe Nick could—

"Oh, it's a real classic," Sarah piped up.

Nicholas glared at her and wondered what the penalty was for murdering your sister. Maybe they'd go easy on him. I mean, who would mind one less big-mouth sister in the world?

She wasn't done, either. In fact, she was grinning. At last her day had meaning: she could go to bed knowing that once again she had ruined Nicholas's entire life. *"Night of the Blood Freaks— Part IV,"* she told their dad, savoring each word.

Slowly Dad straightened up and looked at Nick over the door of the fridge. Nick tried not to let their eyes meet, but it did no good. He looked at his father pitifully, helplessly. "It's in 3-D," he croaked.

"No way. Absolutely not."

"But Dad . . . " Nick could feel himself starting to get angry.

"Honey," Mom reasoned, "we don't want you filling your mind with that kind of garbage. You know that."

Now they were coming at him from both sides. "But Mom . . ."

"I told you so." Sarah couldn't resist getting in another good jab.

Frustrated, Nicholas spun around at her and shouted, "Shut up!"

"Nicholas." Dad's voice was anything but pleased.

"Well . . . ," Nick was stuttering, looking for the right words. "Why am I always the one who can't do anything?" His voice was getting high and shrill, a good sign he was losing control.

"Nicholas . . . ," Dad warned.

But it was all coming out now, and there was nothing Nick could do to stop it. "Can't do this, can't do that—"

"One more word out of you, young man—"

"It's not fair," Nicholas shouted over his dad. "Everybody else gets to go out—"

"Nichol—" Mom tried to stop him from getting in any worse hot water, but Nick was too busy shouting to hear.

"Everybody else gets to go, but I have to sit around with a bunch of old—"

"That's it!" Dad's voice was sharp and to the point. It immediately brought Nicholas to a stop. He'd gone too far and he knew it.

Dad continued firm and even. "We don't talk that way in this home. Now go to your room. You're grounded."

Nicholas couldn't believe his ears. Grounded! How could this have gone so wrong?

He looked at Dad. The man stood solid and firm. Then he looked at his mom. She was also holding her ground.

Nick felt his ears start to burn, his head start to pound. He was so mad he felt like exploding, but what could he do? His dad had spoken. And by the tone in his voice and the look in his eyes, Nick knew he meant every word of it.

Nicholas Martin, Mr. "I-can-handle-my-folks-no-sweat," was grounded—and there was nothing he could do about it.

Finally he snapped around and started for the stairs. It was so unfair. ALL OF IT!

He reached the bottom of the steps and started to stomp up them . . . loudly. He may not be able to say anything more, but no one had said anything about stomping.

Mom and Dad looked on. Neither was happy about having to ground Nicholas. Unfortunately, he'd left them no choice.

FOUR
Everybody's a Critic!

Parents. Yeah, you know who they are. The folks that hang around your house telling you when to walk, talk, and jump—and how high. The big guys who always hand out orders like "Take out the trashEat your vegetablesTake a bathPractice your tubaStop practicing your tubaDon't pick at itChange your socksClean up your roomGet a haircut" . . . and about a thousand other things that you hate to do.

But, hey, they can't help it. That's their job. Everyone knows parents are supposed to make you do all those things and prevent you from having fun.

Oh, yeah. They're best at that . . . at preventing you from having fun. Like when you want to go skateboarding down the freeway with Tom, Dick, and Harry. The answer is always no: "No, you'll get run over. Skateboard around the house where it's safe."

OK, so it's a pain to stay home while Tom, Dick,

and Harry get to skateboard down the freeway. But, hey, like I always say, it's better to stay home than wind up a pancake under some semi's rear tire.

Besides, I've noticed something interesting. Nick's folks usually only put the clamps on him when his "fun" is gonna end up creaming him. I know, it doesn't make being clamped any easier. But I got a pretty good hunch that's how it is with most parents.

Shucks, parents are bound to know something. I don't think you can get that job unless you've been around and learned some things. Unfortunately, convincing my buddy Nick of that wasn't easy.

Dad and Mom had just dropped the big one on Nick's plans for the Night of the Blood Freaks. He had lost the war, big time. Not only was he forbidden to see the gross-out flick with Louis, but his "diplomacy" had landed him in the clink. He came stomping into the bedroom mad at the world, just as I was getting ready for bed and brushing my teeth.

I decided to take pity on my pal, maybe enlighten him in the workings of parent-child relationships. Of course, this meant I was going to have to think like an adult. Not an easy task, but I figured I'd give it a shot.

As Nick wrestled with his shirt and kicked off his shoes, I began my approach. "Hey, Nick," I started off cheerfully.

"Ah, go smell your socks," he barked.

"Wound a bit tightly tonight, aren't we?" I kidded. But he just kept yanking his clothes off as if they were on fire and pounced down on the bed in a boiling heap of frustration. "Look, kid," I said, trying to reason with him. "You watch movies like that long enough and pretty soon they'll stick a sign on your head that says 'dump site.'"

"What are you, some kind of film critic?" he scoffed as he tugged back the covers and crawled into bed.

"Well, as a matter of fact . . . "

Suddenly we were sitting in a deserted theater balcony (ain't imagination grand?). I was crammed into a snug fitting V-neck sweater and an equally tight pair of polyester slacks. Nick was in an open-collar dress shirt and a well fitting navy blazer. We had become the Dynamic Duo of movie criticdom: Roger Beefer and Gene Dismal, the cohosts of TV's "Let's Mangle the Movies."

"Well, Gene," I said, "let's take a look at our next clip, The Molting Falcon. OK, roll it." Nothing happened. "Roll it! Roll it already!"

Finally the screen began to flicker and the movie began. . . .

"My name is Shade," the leading man said (an outstanding award-winning actor who bears an uncanny resemblance to yours truly). "Spam Shade, Private Eye. I was relaxing in my second story office on the lower East Side: the lower, lower East Side. It was so low the snails wore elevator shoes just to stay on the sidewalk. Even so, it wasn't as low as I was feeling.

"I was down. I had been working two weeks, night and day, on a case that was really a tough nut to crack. (Actually, it was a walnut. I'd used a hammer, a pair of pliers, and a screwdriver, and I still hadn't gotten the thing opened. A guy could starve to death. Next Christmas I hoped Aunt Nellie would send me a fruitcake instead.) I sat back in my chair and took a stout swig of my diet soda.

"Then she walked in.

"She stepped into the place like she owned the joint. She leaned against the doorway and drew out a cigarette. I guess she didn't notice the No Smoking sign. Being a gentleman, I was gonna offer her a light. Then I saw she had one. A blow torch.

"She lit up the room. As a matter of fact, she lit up the coatrack. We put the fire out, then I asked her name. 'Thelma,' she said. She was the kind of babe your mom warned you about. That's OK, though. Mom was in Cleveland getting a nose job. So I asked her to take a seat.

"She sat down, then said she was looking for her bird, a molting falcon. She whipped out a half-charred photo and handed it to me. It was a picture of her and the bird standing in front of Old Geezer, the world famous waterspout in Yellow Phones National Park. The bird was wearing a polka-dot tie. It looked like they had been on vacation. . . . I was beginning to think they were also out to lunch.

"Thelma said the bird had disappeared around the docks. She thought the whole thing smelled kind of fishy. I wondered what she expected the docks to smell like.

"Well, it just so happened I had been down at the docks earlier and found just such a bird. I whipped it out of my drawer. The tie matched and so did the bird. Too bad it was dead now.

"Just then I heard a blood-curdling scream accompanied by a loud thud. It was Thelma, passed out on the floor. I guess she was the sensitive type. Either that or it was time for her afternoon nap.

"Oh well, that wraps up another thrilling case for Spam Shade, Private Eye."

The lights in the theater came up and I turned to my partner. "You know, Gene," I said, "they just don't make films like that anymore. Great story, great dialogue—and a particularly great performance by the lead. I give this flick a thumbs up."

"No way," Roger said. "If that film was any flatter it would be in the House of Pancakes. Now if you want to see a really great flick, let's take a look at the new remake, starring that action-packed performer, Flint Streethood. OK, roll it."

Now folks, as near as I can tell, this film had something to do with somebody being mad at somebody about something, and it's just as well you never see it. Still, let me see if I can describe what happened.

Some guy carrying a gun the size of a B-52 bomber walked into a drugstore and said, "OK, punk, make my parfait." The next thing I know everybody was shooting at everybody else. It went something like this:

Kapow! Kapow! Blam! Blam! Whir! Bang! Bang! Bang! Rat-tat-tat-tat-tat-tat-tat-tat! Kaboom! Kawham! Bang! Cough! Cough! Kak-kak-kak-kak! Wheeze! Wheeze! Kagang! Kagang! Whir! Whir! Pop!

Are you getting the idea? The last thing I remember was a grenade coming straight out of the screen and . . . KaWHOOM!

"You call that fun?!" I gasped. The blast had blown us clear out of our make-believe theater and back to the bedroom—which was fine with me. "Why don't you just stick your head in a garbage can?"

"Because then I would have to room with you," Nick said with a cough as he reached for the light next to the bedpost. "Let's just try to get some sleep."

Well, at least he's forgotten about the silly Blood Freak flick, *I thought.* Then again, who knows? Tomorrow is another day, and boys will be boys. Or will they?

FIVE
Cyborg's Plan

By 9:00 the next morning things had started to look a little better. Not perfect, mind you, but a little better. For starters, it was Saturday. And Saturday meant, you guessed it, no school!

It's not that Nicholas hated school. It's just that he could think of a lot better ways to spend six hours a day. Which according to his calculations meant:

6 hours x 5 days=30 hours a week!

30 hours x 4 weeks=120 hours a month!

120 hours x 9 months=1,080 hours a year!

1,080 HOURS A YEAR IN SCHOOL! Awful! Terrible! Of course, Nick ignored the fact that the only reason he could do those calculations was because he had spent so much time in school.

Anyway, another reason Saturday morning looked better was that Nick had cooled down some. As usual, his talk with McGee had helped. Not that he agreed with the little munchkin. Hardly. But he was able to understand a little more where his folks were coming from. Only a little, though.

Another good thing was the news on Whatever. The vet called bright and early that morning to say everything was fine. There was no need to operate. In fact, they could pick him up anytime they wanted.

Of course, Sarah had her dad talked into going down there in no time flat. She was feeling pretty good. In fact, she was feeling so good that she started to make excuses about giving Whatever the bone. They were barely out of the garage before she had herself convinced that it wasn't even her fault.

"I was just doing the loving thing," she insisted. "You couldn't expect me to be some mean old ogre and say no, could you? I mean, not when I love him?"

Dad could only shake his head at her logic. "It's because you love him that I'd expect you to say no," he explained.

Sarah looked at him, confused.

"Sweetheart," he continued, "just because you love someone doesn't always mean you let him have his way. I mean, look at Nicholas."

"I'd rather not," she cracked.

Dad ignored the comment. "Nick wanted to see that movie—but we knew it was bad for him."

"You mean with all the blood and gore and junk."

"Right. Seeing that movie would be as bad for Nick's mind as that chicken bone was for Whatever's stomach."

"OK . . . so . . . "

"So," Dad continued, "which would have shown

him more love? Letting him go off and do something that would hurt him, or saying no and letting him be angry at us?"

"I guess saying no."

Dad nodded.

Sarah was starting to see the picture . . . and for once she didn't have a comeback. Well, she always had a comeback. This one just wasn't great. "It's hard to say no," she insisted. "I mean, you know how Whatever loves chicken."

"It's hard for us to say no to you guys, too. If we had it our way we'd always say yes. We'd always give you what you wanted. But we see the bigger picture, and because we love you . . . well, sometimes we have to be the heavy and say no."

Sarah looked out the window. After a long moment she said, "Being a parent doesn't always sound so easy."

"No kidding!" Dad exclaimed.

Sarah turned back to him and grinned. "It does have its rewards, though, doesn't it?"

A puzzled look came across his face. "Gee," he said, "if you hear of any, let me know."

"Daddy!" Sarah gave him a poke in the ribs and he broke into a grin.

It's too bad Nicholas hadn't heard that conversation. Maybe his decision would have been different when Louis called. . . .

"Hello?"

"Hey, Nick." Louis's voice was a little thick and raspy from the morning, but Nicholas immediately recognized it. "You ready for the flick?"

Oh no, Nick thought. He'd forgotten all about his promise to Louis. Not only would he have to explain why he couldn't go, but now he'd have to go through all of Louis's jabs and jokes about how strict his parents were. To make it worse, his mother was standing three feet away at the kitchen sink. Well, better to get it over with, quick and simple. . . .

"I can't go."

"What?" Louis asked.

"I'm grounded."

"Grounded?" Louis knew Nick's parents were strict—but not that strict. "How are you going to the show if you're grounded?"

"I can't."

"Oh, man . . . ," Louis sighed.

It wasn't easy for Mom to hear this conversation. She knew how important the movie was to Nick. She could tell how embarrassed he was. Still . . . she also knew how rude he'd been the night before. Even more important, she knew how harmful the movie would be.

Unfortunately, the wheels inside Louis's brain were turning. An idea was coming to his beady little brain. "Hold it . . . Wait a minute," he said. "Wait a minute . . . 'Blue Fox Leader.'"

"Huh?" Nick didn't get it. What did the TV series have to do with him being grounded? How was that going to help him see the movie?

"Remember last week's episode?" Louis asked. "Remember the plan Cyborg II used to free Blue Fox from the dreaded Black Tower?"

It took Nicholas a moment to catch on. Then he

remembered the show . . . he remembered how
Cyborg and Blue Fox used their telecommunicators,
how Cyborg distracted the Scorpion-tailed android
guards so Blue Fox could make his escape. Most important, he remembered how Blue Fox used his superior creativity to build a decoy.

"Superior creativity. Hmmmmm." That was right
up Nicholas's alley. He cast a guarded look at his
mom, and slid out of earshot as he and Louis
worked out their plan. . . .

First Nick attached the toilet plunger.

It took some doing, but with Crazy Glue and the
right amount of suction Nick was able to make it
stick onto the inside of his bedroom door.

Next came the electrical cable. Sure, it looked
like a lot of twisted-up Christmas tree lights. And
he probably didn't need them all blinking. But,
hey, that was part of the effect. He hooked one
end of the cable to a small sensor on the plunger.
Then he attached the other end to a cassette
player on his bed.

Now for the recorded message. Nick was careful
to make his voice sound just bored enough.

For the normal kid, this stuff would be pretty
hard to do. Nicholas, however, was no normal kid.
He had this imagination that just wouldn't stop.
You could see it in all of his McGee drawings. You
could see it in his automatic walnut cracker. You
could see it in his light-activated door opener.
Today, though, he'd outdone himself. Today he'd
created the "Fool-your-parents-so-they-think-
you're-still-in-your-room" invention.

The last step was the light bulb. He screwed it into the socket attached to the plunger. Then Nick hesitated for a moment. This was it. Would it really work? He took a deep breath and gently knocked on the door.

The bulb lit up! It was a success! ALL RIGHT!

It had taken him nearly two hours. Two hours of rummaging for parts in the garage, the basement, the attic . . . and then there were all those delicate electrical hookups. Finally, though, he was finished. And it actually worked!

Just in time, too. Almost immediately his walkie-talkie began to beep. It had to be Louis.

Nicholas picked it up and said, "Cyborg II, this is Blue Fox Leader. Do you copy?"

For a moment there was no answer and Nick's heart began to sink. Without Louis the plan would not work. Without Louis he couldn't possibly sneak out. Without Louis—

"Roger, Blue Fox. I'm reading you loud and clear."

Nick broke into a grin.

Louis was outside hiding in the front yard. He was trying his best to look like the super-intelligent and ever-so-wise Cyborg II. Unfortunately he didn't quite make it.

Maybe it was his clothes. Maybe it was the pulled-down stocking cap, the thick scarf, and the heavy sweatshirt. Or maybe it was all the sweat he was covered with from wearing those clothes in 80-degree weather. In any case, Louis looked more like a crazed bag lady than the all-knowing hero from Kalugrium.

That didn't stop him, though. Not one bit. Fantasy was fantasy, and he planned to play this one to the hilt.

"Synchronize watches to 11:28," Louis continued, "and let's commence execution."

"Execution?" The word caught Nicholas off guard. Until now it had all been fun and games, it really hadn't been real . . . but "execution" sounded an awful lot like punishment. And punishment would definitely be a part of Nick's future if he were caught. After all, he was disobeying his parents . . . and in a *big* way.

Reality only lasted a second, though. Louis soon brought Nick back to his senses.

"Yeah. Execute the plan. You know, 'the plan.' "

"Oh, uh, right . . . the plan."

Nicholas grinned as he pushed down the antenna and threw on his coat. Everything was going great! Everything had been worked out. There would be no problems.

Or so he thought. . . .

Tsk, tsk, tsk . . . "What a tangled web we weave when we prac-i-tac-ice to deceive." That's what I always say. And that's exactly what my good buddy Nick was doing. He thought he was being quite the clever escape artist with all those electronic gizmos and wires running every which way.

I must admit his creativity in the matter was quite impressive. His electronic doodads gave a realistic impression that he was calmly sketching in his room. Well, everybody else might be fooled, but not me.

I don't know. It seemed like a lot of wasted effort to fake his parents out just so he could go and be grossed out. Why didn't he just go downstairs and make a broccoli and stewed prune sandwich? Always works for me.

Besides, seems to me Nick should devote his time to more rewarding activities. You know, challenging endeavors that would spark his mind and spirit. Things that would help him be a better person. Things like . . . well, you know . . . like clipping his toenails.

Yeah. That's it. If he would clip his toenails on a regular basis, it would . . . well, it would . . . OK, it wouldn't do anything. But since it was what I was doing at the time, I thought it was pretty worthwhile.

Still, as preoccupied with that task as I was (after all, I didn't want to cut off my big toe or something), I decided it was time to tell Nick how I felt about his little rendezvous with Louis. "You'll be sorry," I said, continuing to trim away at my tootsies.

"Aren't you coming?" Nick asked.

Obviously, he knew if I played along with his clever little scheme, he'd have a better chance of pulling it off. But I didn't want any part of it. "Uh-uh, no way," I said in a superior tone. "I got principles. I got convictions. . . ." I leaped to my feet and began to sing, "I got rhythm. . . ."

But Nick wasn't the least bit impressed. He just stood there for a second, until a sly grin crossed his face. He had an idea, I could tell. But it wouldn't work. No matter what he said, I was going to make him realize how I felt about this whole under-handed plot. Nothing was going to change my mind. So I just kept on singing, "I got rhythm. . . ."

"I'll give you a dollar," he offered.

"I got . . . to get my shoes," I said.

OK, so I gave in. Can I help it if I was flat busted and would do anything for a buck? Well, at least I'll have a little walking money for the show, I thought. Although all you can get at the movies for a buck these days is a cup of ice and half a Milk Dud.

Nick made some final adjustments on his "Fool-your-folks" invention while I laced up my glow-in-the-dark tennis shoes. (I like to see where I'm walking in those dark theaters.)

We both stood there a second, took a deep breath, then cautiously crept out the bedroom door.

I sure hoped this stupid plan worked. Or we would end up in worse shape than any of the victims in this freak flick ever thought about. . . .

SIX
The Escape!

Carefully Blue Fox ("Nick" to his friends) moved down the stairs. Who knew where his enemies lurked? Who knew what dastardly tortures he would face if caught? It didn't matter, though, for his courage was great. Yes, the courage of Blue Fox Leader was beyond compare.

Unfortunately, there was only one way out—through the Control Center of the enemy's fortress (which, to untrained eyes, looked a lot like a kitchen).

Thanks to months of training, Blue Fox knew exactly which steps creaked and which didn't. With expert wisdom he avoided those hidden alarms, which had obviously been placed by the enemy to alert them in case he tried to escape.

As he approached the Control Center, he could hear the murmur of an alien voice. With each step the voice grew louder. By its higher pitch, Blue Fox could tell it was the Female Unit, the second in command. Fortunately, the Supreme Commander was out back spray-painting some patio furniture.

Carefully Blue Fox peeked around the corner of the stairs. There she was . . . the Female. She was talking on the phone to the counseling center. Across the counter in the family room, Blue Fox could see the Female Unit's mother. They called her Grandma for short. She had her back to him and was knitting. Probably some phaser-proof vest for one of the Offspring.

Ah, yes. The Offspring!

Quickly Blue Fox scanned the area. Fortunately the Offspring were nowhere to be found. Good. Well, good and bad. Good because it meant Blue Fox would not have to sneak past them. (The Offsprings' senses were much keener than those of the Older Units.) Bad because the Offspring were just the kind of creatures who would suddenly swoop in from nowhere and catch him out in the open.

This was not a time for fear, though. This was a time for action. Blue Fox knew he had to cross the Control Center. That meant the Female Unit must be removed. Blue Fox pulled back out of sight. Quietly he keyed in his telecommunicator.

"Cyborg II, Cyborg II, this is Blue Fox Leader," he whispered. "Emergency at kitchen. Request diversionary tactic."

Louis was still outside hiding in the front yard when his buddy's call for help came. All right! This is what he'd been waiting for! He answered, "Roger, Blue Fox. I'm on my way."

Like a shot, he jumped up from behind the concrete wall and headed for the front porch. It was a dangerous mission. Any moment he could be spotted by the enemy and demolecularized (you know, melted into a little puddle of loose atoms). That didn't matter, though, because that was his friend in there. That was the great Blue Fox Leader. And if there was one thing Cyborg II was famous for it was his loyalty.

Inside, Blue Fox pressed himself flat against the stairway wall and waited. Would Cyborg II complete his mission?

It had been tricky, and Cyborg II had had more than one close call. Finally, though, he reached the stairs of the front porch. Just in time, too, for a motorized vehicle (that earthlings would call a "car") came cruising around the corner. Cyborg II dropped behind the bushes out of sight as it passed.

Then, summoning all his strength and courage, Cyborg II rose from hiding, glanced about, and raced up the stairs toward the front door, where he reached out and began to ring the doorbell . . . once, twice. Then he darted down the steps as quickly as he had come.

When he heard the doorbell, Blue Fox grinned. Cyborg II had not let him down. Furthermore, the plan had the desired effect upon the Female Unit.

"Uh, Mary Ann?" the Female Unit said over the phone. "Can you hold on? There's somebody at the door."

Blue Fox heard her set the phone down on the

counter and push open the hallway door. Perfect!

Now it was time to make his move!

He started across the kitchen, planning to go through the family room and out the other door. With any luck he'd go completely undetected.

So much for luck. . . .

"Sarah . . . ," he heard the Female Unit call from the hallway. "Can you see who that is at the door?" Then the hallway door started to open.

Oh no! What should he do!? The Female Unit was coming back in and he was trapped out in the open! Then he spotted it—the control console, cleverly disguised as one of those stove tops built in the middle of the kitchen. It wasn't very big, but it would have to do. He dove for cover just as the door opened.

Blue Fox held his breath, waiting. He was crouched on one side of the little kitchen island and the Female Unit was standing on the other. They were less than four feet apart.

She picked up the phone and started talking again. For a moment, Blue Fox was safe. Well, not quite. True to form, the Female Unit liked to keep busy. There was a long cord on the phone, so she could move all around the kitchen as she talked.

Suddenly Blue Fox heard her approaching footsteps. Oh no! She was heading right for him! Quickly he scrambled on his hands and knees to the opposite side.

He made it just as she rounded the corner. It was close, but he was safe.

Well, not quite.

Suddenly the Female Unit changed directions

and headed the opposite way. Blue Fox frantically switched into reverse and backed up. Then she changed direction again, and so did he. It looked like some strange sort of dance as she unknowingly chased him around the little island . . . first one direction, than the other, and then the first direction again.

Blue Fox Leader was beginning to feel a little ridiculous . . . not to mention a lot dizzy.

Finally the Female Unit finished her conversation and hung up the phone. Then Blue Fox Leader heard it . . . that wonderful sound of the squeaky kitchen door being opened again.

"Sarah?" the Female Unit called. "Sarah, who was at the door?"

Perfect! She was out of the room. Blue Fox rose to his feet and started for the family room door, only to dive again for cover as the Offspring threw it open. "Mother?"

Now Blue Fox was at the end of the kitchen counter—the one that separated the kitchen from the family room. And if that wasn't bad enough, the Female Unit suddenly came back through the kitchen door. "Oh, there you are."

What is this, a convention? Blue Fox thought. It was crazy. The Female Unit was on one side of the counter and the Offspring was on the other. While he, the great Blue Fox Leader, was trapped in between. All either one of them had to do was cross three feet down his way, and bingo, they'd spot him.

"Who was at the door?" the Female Unit asked.

"No one," the Offspring answered.

"Probably one of those screwy kids."

"But Mom," the Offspring argued. "Nicholas is upstairs."

For a moment Nick thought it was unfair that the real Blue Fox Leader didn't have to put up with a sister.

"Grandma?" The Offspring turned toward the sofa to speak with the Older Unit. "Can you help me with the curtains in my room?"

"Well, sure, Dear," the Older Unit answered.

Blue Fox heard the creak of the sofa as she rose to her feet. "How do they look?" she asked. "Is the length OK?"

Great! They were heading toward the door.

"Well, kind of," the Offspring answered. "But it's uneven at the bottom."

"We'll take care of that," the Older Unit said as the door creaked open and their voices faded down the hall.

Super! Now it was just Blue Fox and the Female Unit!

He leaned back and looked over his shoulder. She was at the counter starting to make some peanut butter and jelly nutrition packets. Silently, he dropped to his knees and inched his way around to the family room side of the counter.

The doorway lay just ahead. All he had to do was quietly crawl toward the door. . . .

Carefully he crept forward. Foot by foot, inch by inch. All the time he could hear the Female Unit just above his head, on the other side, preparing the meal. Closer and closer the door came. He was nearly there.

A good thing, too. The game was starting to wear on Nicholas. It had started off fun enough . . . but all this sneaking, this hiding, this disobeying . . . well, it was definitely starting to take its toll on him. A tight little knot of guilt had started growing in his stomach, and it was growing bigger by the second.

Finally he reached his hand out to the door. Soon it would be over. Then the worst happened. He was spotted—by a four-legged hairball. It was the Offspring's pesky pooch! And worse yet, the carnivorous canine thought Blue Fox wanted to play. So he began to bark.

Blue Fox tried to shush him. He tried to silence him. The animal just took it as signs of encouragement. He'd just spent the last twelve hours at the vet's teetering between life and Poochie Paradise. Now that he was OK, he figured it was time to party. So he barked even louder.

"What on earth?" the Female Unit leaned over the counter toward the dog. She was directly above Blue Fox's head, but could not see him. "Whatever, are you all right, boy?"

The dog continued to bark.

"Whatever . . . what's wrong, fella?" Her voice sounded more concerned.

Oh no! Any minute she'd set down her knife and cross into the family room to check out the problem. Maybe she thought he was still sick. Maybe she thought he was having a relapse. Either way, once she crossed around the counter she would spot the great Blue Fox Leader!

Desperately, Blue Fox looked for a solution.

Anything . . . he'd even settle for a chicken bone right now. There was nothing.

Well . . . almost nothing. . . .

Have you ever noticed this? That in the most critical moment of a daring and dangerous escape plan, when the safety of the entire free world rides on split-second timing, there's always some mangy mutt hanging around who starts barking his head off? Which, of course, alerts everyone from Cleveland to Crabwell Corners of your presence. Have you ever noticed that?

It happens every time. In fact, it was happening right now to my good buddy, Nick.

Whatever, the family fur ball, was only seconds away from blowing our movie mission. The half-witted hound's persistent barking had to go, otherwise Nicholas would probably replace this pooch in the doghouse.

What old Rover needed was a little game of fetch, commando style. I whipped out a nice, round, black bomb, which I keep for such occasions, and lit the fuse. Nick gave me a look of alarm. I think he was afraid I was about to give this pup a permanent toothache. Of course, that wasn't the plan.

I gave Nick a reassuring wink, then beckoned to Whatever with the burning bomb. "Come here, boy," I called, slapping my thigh and giving a soft whistle, waving the bomb around like a fine turkey bone.

The dorky dog stopped barking and stepped forward hesitantly. Hooray for curiosity.

I continued to sweet-talk the critter, until he finally

sniffed at the fizzling fuse. Just as I had hoped, a
spark flew out and smacked Whatever right on the
nose. The chickenhearted cat-chaser turned tail and
raced through the kitchen and up the stairs, yelping
all the way.

Mom, somewhat startled, dropped what she was
doing and followed in hot pursuit. "Whatever, are
you OK? Come here. Come here, fellow. Whatever?"

Nick heaved a sigh of relief. "Thanks," he
whispered.

I licked my fingers and pinched out the burning
fuse. "It will cost you another seventy-five cents," I
said calmly.

Nick looked annoyed. But, hey, that had been a
pretty desperate situation. Besides, the extra cash
would come in handy at the show. Now I could get
a whole Milk Dud.

Nick rose to his feet, shot a glance around the
room, then crept out of the kitchen. "Let's go," he
whispered to me over his shoulder.

This movie had better be worth it, I thought as I
followed him out of the kitchen. Or I'm going to
charge him another quarter when we get home.

By the time Nick made it outside, he was ex-
hausted. All that sneaking around had worn him
out. Besides, that little knot of guilt in his
stomach was now about the size of a baseball.
Needless to say, he was glad the game was finally
over.

Well, almost.

Louis was still wearing his stocking cap. His
scarf was still pulled up over his face and he was

still using their walkie-talkie. Nick may have been done with the game, but Louis had only begun.

"C'mon," Louis whispered. "Follow me."

Nicholas glanced around. "Why are we whispering?"

"Shhhh."

Louis turned—and fell over the garbage cans beside them. They clanked and rattled and banged, making all sorts of racket. Some of the neighborhood dogs started barking.

The two boys pressed flat against the wall just as Mom stuck her head out the front door to have a look. She saw nothing.

"Strange," she said as she finally turned to shut the door. "Very strange."

The boys relaxed, but Nick's heart was beating like a jackhammer. Louis glanced around, then turned to Nicholas and whispered, "Meet me over by that Buick."

"Louis," Nicholas sighed. "Let's just go to the theater." He was sick of the game . . . and he was sick of all the guilt he was feeling.

"What are you talking about?" Louis demanded. "That's not what Blue Fox would do."

"No, and Blue Fox's mom wouldn't chase him around the kitchen either."

"Let's just stick to the plan," Louis urged. With that he dashed off.

Nicholas swallowed hard. He wanted to be a good sport, but he also wanted to get rid of the guilt he was feeling. I mean, here his folks were trusting him, expecting him to obey . . . and look what he was doing. It felt terrible. That baseball

lying in his stomach was now the size of a volleyball. He took a deep breath, muttered something about not remembering a Buick in the plan,
and finally took off.

SEVEN
Attack of the Blood Freaks

The boys had plenty of time to walk to the theater.
But superheros never walk. They "dash," "dart," or
"zip." So Louis made sure they did just that . . . all
the way.

By the time they finally reached the theater,
Nicholas wasn't sure if the pain in his gut was
from the guilt or from all the running. Either way,
it felt bad. And it was getting worse.

Finally, there it was. The theater. And up on the
marquee, in vivid glorious red, was the title, *Night
of the Blood Freaks, Part IV.*

Nicholas swallowed hard. He had come this far.
There was no backing out now. Then a thought
struck him.

"Wait a minute, Louis," he said. "How are we
supposed to get in if we're not old enough?"

Not to worry. The great Cyborg II had already figured out a plan. "No problem," he said with a grin.
"Follow me." With that, he took off for the ticket
line.

Nicholas swallowed again. By this time, though, there wasn't much left to swallow. His mouth was as dry as the Sahara desert. Numbly, he turned and followed his friend to the back of the line.

Interestingly enough, the back of the line doesn't stay the back of the line forever. Nick saw that they were moving closer and closer toward the box office window. Any second they'd be there. Any second Nick's crime would be found out. Any second the SWAT teams would appear, arrest him, and throw him in jail for life. Or, worse yet, he'd be forced to listen to one of his dad's lectures.

Closer and closer they came. Why had he agreed to this? What had he been thinking of?

Now the man in front of them stepped up to the window. He was average looking—Greek or maybe Arab. Not a bad sort of fellow. He paid for his ticket and moved off.

It was their turn.

Nicholas looked up to the box office attendant. She was kind of pretty, but he didn't notice. He was paralyzed. He couldn't move. He couldn't speak.

Fortunately, Louis could. And he did. Beautifully. "Two, please?" he asked. Then turning to the man who had just left he called out, "Wait up . . . Dad."

A stroke of genius! A brilliant plan! In one sentence Louis had solved all of their problems. Those three little words would get them in, free and clear. Fantastic! Except for one minor problem . . . "Dad" was Greek, Louis was black.

The box office attendant frowned down at them.

Always thinking, Louis pointed to Nicholas. "His dad," he said, reaching in to grab the tickets and head after the man.

"Whew, that was close," Louis whispered to Nicholas . . . but Nicholas was not there. He was still frozen in front of the box office, a pathetic little smile pasted on his face.

Louis took a step back, grabbed him by the collar, and yanked him toward the door.

Back at home Mom was feeling pretty proud of her son. Nick had taken his punishment so well. He really was a wonderful kid. Not one word of complaint from him all morning. In fact, she hadn't heard any word from him for several hours. She decided to swing up to his room and say hi, and tell him how proud she was of him. Then maybe, just maybe, the whole family could go out later and do something together. Maybe pizza. Maybe miniature golf. Maybe both.

She knocked gently on his door and waited.

Her "wonderful" son's little invention—the one he had spent so much time hooking up—finally went into operation.

Mom's knock started it all by lighting up the light on the door. This sent electricity down the long cable of Christmas tree lights to the cassette recorder. The power snapped the recorder on play and suddenly Mom heard Nick's voice—recorded, but loud and clear: "Who is it?"

"It's Mom," she said from the other side.

"I'm drawing right now," Nick's voice said. "Could you come back later?"

"All right, Hon," Mom said, and she left his door with a smile.

What a terrific kid. Other children might have sulked or stayed mad. Not Nicholas. He took his medicine like a real trooper. What a kid. What a delight.

Mom moved down the hall beaming with pride.

Well, Nicholas was taking his medicine all right. Just not exactly the way Mom thought. . . .

At first things in the theater were OK. Nick had never worn 3-D glasses before, and it was pretty exciting the way the credits seemed to jump off the screen at him. For a few moments the ache in his gut was almost gone and he was actually glad he'd come.

Then the movie started.

The mutants weren't so bad to look at. In fact, it was kind of fun to watch the way they hobbled across the lawn. And their mutant-type of noises were more disgusting than scary. It was when they got into the house . . . and what they did there . . . well, at first it was kind of interesting. Then it got gross. Then, when you were sure it couldn't get any worse . . . it did.

Nick glanced at Louis. It was hard to see his friend's expression behind those 3-D glasses. Still, Louis was definitely feeling something. I mean, the kid was munching down popcorn faster than Nick had ever seen him eat in his life.

It had been nearly half an hour since Mom checked in on Nicholas. She had just gone up-stairs to put

away laundry, so she figured she'd stop by and give another knock.

"Who is it?" the recorded voice asked. Only this time it started to drag, which made Nick's voice sound very low and slow. Apparently, Nick had forgotten one small element in his perfect plan: he hadn't checked the batteries in the cassette player.

Mom frowned. "Honey, it's Mom. Are you OK? You sound . . . ," she searched for the right word, "tired."

No answer.

"Nicholas?"

She knocked again.

Still no answer.

"Nicholas?" Her concern started to grow. She knocked harder, which shook the cables attached to the recorder, which made the delicate little connectors shake loose and short out—which tripped the cassette player into the "record" mode.

"Nicholas, it's Mom. What's going on in there?" More knocking. More shaking. The recorder clicked back into the "play" mode.

Finally, Mom heard an answer from the other side of the door—but not the one she was expecting. "It's Mom," the voice said, "what's going on in there?"

Mom stopped a moment. That sounded like *her* voice. Not only did it sound like her voice . . . it *was* her voice.

Sarah stuck her head out of her room to see what the fuss was about. "Hey, Mom, what're you doing?"

"What's it look like I'm doing?" she said. "I'm talking to myself."

They looked at each other. Something was wrong. Something was definitely wrong.

Then, from the other side of Nick's door, they heard Mom's voice again: "What's it look like I'm doing? I'm talking to myself."

That did it. Mom turned the knob and threw open the door. "Nicholas, what on earth . . . ?"

There was no Nicholas. There was only her recorded voice, saying "Nicholas, what on earth" at about three different speeds.

The cable attached to the light. The cassette player attached to the cable. Yes, indeed, another one of Nicholas's marvelous inventions.

At first Mom didn't understand. Then it began to make sense. It was all a trick. A sneaky trick to make them think he was in his room.

But why? Why would Nicholas want to deceive them like this?

She looked around the room and spotted the answer. On the bed. It was the newspaper advertisement for *Night of the Blood Freaks, Part IV.*

Mom was not smiling.

Back at the theater the Blood Freaks had found the family and begun attacking them . . . one at a time. The sounds were awful . . . lots of screaming, and choking, and gagging. But the sounds were nothing compared to what you watched. What Nicholas watched. What he couldn't take his eyes from.

As he watched, that volleyball come back into his stomach. Only now it wasn't content just to stay in his stomach. It was trying to jump up his throat and out his mouth. Nicholas tried his best to swallow it . . . but the worse the movie got, the harder it was to keep it down.

Finally everybody was killed off. Well, almost everybody. There was still one little member left. The tiny little sister. She cried, she whimpered, she begged . . . but nothing stopped the Blood Freaks. They did to her what they did to the others. Only worse. Much worse. Much, much worse. Worse than much worse.

Then, just when Nick thought they had finished—just when he reached for his soda and tried to take a sip from his straw to settle his stomach—the Freaks finished their attack with this sickening slurp that sounded just like a soda straw getting the last little bit of drink in a cup.

Nick looked at his straw. Suddenly he wasn't so thirsty anymore. . . .

EIGHT
Busted

At last the nightmare was over. The credits ended, and the final words on the screen were:

"Coming soon to a blood bank near you . . . *Blood Feast of the Blood Freaks—Part V.*"

The kids in the audience broke into cheers. Nick couldn't believe it. He glanced around. Everybody looked as sick and pale as he felt. They were wiped out, too . . . but they were still cheering and clapping. It was like they could hardly wait to get grossed out all over again.

"Great flick, huh?" Louis beamed.

Nick tried to smile, but he wasn't too successful. Louis saw it, and for a second his grin also faded. For a second Nick could see what his friend was really thinking. Louis wasn't feeling so swift either. It lasted only a second, though.

"Hey, Louis," one of the kids from behind poked him in the back. "Wasn't that great the way they got that last kid?"

"Yeah." Louis was grinning again. "Or the way they . . ."

Nick didn't hear the rest of the conversation. Louis joined his friends and headed up the aisle. Everyone was laughing and talking and shouting. Nick just shook his head. No one would admit how frightened or scared they were. It was almost like they were trying too hard to prove they had had a good time.

But Nicholas couldn't fake it. He felt terrible. What had he done? And more important, why had he done it? His folks were right. The show was awful. It was worse than awful. It was garbage. First-rate, triple-A garbage . . . with a lot of blood thrown in to wash it down.

The walk home took forever. Unfortunately forever wasn't quite long enough. . . .

When Nick rounded the corner of his block, he quickly checked his front yard. No one was there. So far, so good.

He reached the front porch and quietly crept up the steps. At the door he gave a careful listen. Nothing. The coast was clear. Maybe he could make it back up to his room without being noticed.

He opened the door. It gave a little squeak, but not much. He silently moved down the hall toward the stairs.

Then he spotted it.

It was on the kitchen table, and it wasn't good. There, piled in humiliation, were his cables, his tape recorder, and all of his other electronic gizmos.

The jig was up.

"Nicholas?" It was Dad. He was sitting in the

family room. Apparently he had heard the squeaky door. At that moment, Nick hated that door. His dad's voice was cool and collected. Too cool and collected. "Come in here," he ordered.

Nicholas swallowed hard and obeyed. Slowly, though . . . very slowly.

"Sit down."

There was no mistaking that tone of voice. That was the tone that said, "I'm not going to yell, I'm not going to holler. I'm going to deal with this in a quiet, civilized manner." In other words Nick was going to get it, and he was going to get it good.

If that wasn't bad enough, there was Mom. She was sitting across the coffee table pretending to read her *Ladies' Home Journal.* However, by the way she was flipping through the pages, you knew she wasn't really seeing them. In fact, she wasn't really seeing anything—except red.

"Were you at the movies?" Dad asked.

For the briefest second Nick thought about lying. He could say he'd heard about a gigantic traffic accident on the radio . . . that he'd run downtown to give all the victims mouth-to-mouth resuscitation and save hundreds of lives. Or he could say that, out his window, he'd seen a jet airliner lose its wing in the air . . . and he'd raced to the airport to talk the pilot down to a safe landing. Or maybe they'd believe he had suddenly found a cure for cancer and had to rush down to the hospital so not one more life would be lost.

All these thoughts flashed through his mind in a few seconds. But Nick decided the truth would be better. He'd done enough deceiving for one day.

Besides, if he told the truth maybe they'd let him off easy. You know, something light like life imprisonment.

"Yes sir," he answered his dad's question, barely above a whisper.

"Did you enjoy yourself?" his dad asked.

Again it was time for the truth. "No sir . . . it was awful."

Mom and Dad exchanged looks.

Finally Mom spoke up. "Do you realize what you've done?" she asked.

Nicholas couldn't look up. He couldn't look into their eyes. He could only look at the ground.

"Son . . . ," it was Dad now. "When your mother and I said you couldn't see that movie, we had a purpose."

Nick wanted to say something. He wanted to say that he understood now, that he knew their purpose. But no words came to mind. There was nothing but a tightness forming in the back of his throat. A tightness he couldn't swallow away.

"We wanted to protect you," Mom said.

"Nicholas. Look at me," Dad said quietly. "Nicholas."

It was hard, but at last the boy raised his head. He knew that what his dad was about to say was very important. He knew he'd better hear every word.

"Son," Dad continued. "Your mind is the most important thing you have. That's why the Lord is so clear when he tells us to be careful what we put into it."

The boy continued to hold his dad's gaze. He

would not, could not, look away.

Dad continued. "Whether you enjoyed the show or not is beside the point. By going to see it, you've allowed something to come into your mind . . . to corrupt it . . . to dirty it."

Nick knew exactly what Dad meant. Boy, did he know.

Then it was Mom's turn. "There are scenes inside you now that you'll never be able to erase," she said. Nick could tell how much this upset her by the sad tone of her voice. "Pictures that may stay with you the rest of your life."

Suddenly Nick's eyes started to burn. He wanted to say something. He wanted to let them know what he was feeling. But there were only two words that came to mind. Two words that captured what he felt about disobeying them, about deceiving them, and about seeing the movie . . .

"I'm sorry," he whispered hoarsely.

There was a moment of silence. They knew he meant it. Finally Dad answered. "I'm sorry, too, Son." Another moment. Then Dad continued. "Now I want you to go to your room and give this some thought. I'll be up in a little while to talk about your punishment."

Nicholas nodded slightly and rose to his feet. The movie had been awful, there was no doubt about that. What had been even more awful, though, was knowing how he'd disappointed his parents, how he'd let them down. As he turned, hot tears spilled onto his cheeks.

His back was to Mom and Dad, so they couldn't see his face . . . but it wouldn't have mattered.

They were too busy fighting back the moisture in their own eyes to have seen his.

Being a kid is tough, there's no doubt about it. Being a parent who loves your child enough to do what's best—even when it hurts both of you—well, that's probably even tougher.

NINE
Wrapping Up

Been many a day since he's seen the sun,
got no time to play,
got no time for fun.
'Cause he's having to pay for the things he's done.
Quiet as a mouse.
When Mom and Dad said no,
snuck out to see a scary show.
That's how he found out
Ya reap what ya sow.

The following week found us reaping the "rewards"
of our caper. As punishment for sneaking out of the
house, Nick had to do various chores around the
house.

He was in the middle of hauling a big load of
boxes up to the attic when he stopped in the
kitchen for a well-deserved drink. I, of course, was
helping out by taking the demanding job of "Chief
Supervisor in Charge of Personnel." I had posi-
tioned myself atop the kitchen table. Someone had

to make sure the box hauling journey from the garage to the attic went smoothly for my young friend.

As Nick downed a second glass of water, I tightened the straps on my work gloves and hitched up my support belt another notch. (You can never be too careful when it comes to hard physical labor.)

"Whew! I need a break," Nick said, wiping his brow and setting the glass down on the table.

"So, are we finished?" I asked.

"No, we are not finished. I still have to haul the rest of these boxes from the garage to the attic."

Despite his tone of voice, I knew Nick was really glad to have my help. He just doesn't show his feelings that much.

"Boy, the folks are riding you kind of hard, aren't they?" I commented.

"It could be worse," Nick said. "I could have to sit through that stupid movie again."

We both laughed. Sitting through that movie had been the most agonizing two hours of our lives (except maybe for the time we had to go to the aluminum siding and storm door expo with Mr. Dad). Anyway, hauling boxes was a picnic by comparison.

"I tell you, McGee, I'm through watching garbage like that," Nick said. I smiled. The experiences of the last few days had really taught him a valuable lesson. "But you gotta help me," he added. "That kind of stuff is all around."

Of course, I would be glad to help my little pal. After all it's easier to stick to your guns when

you've got somebody standing beside you.

"Yeah, it's tough making the right choices," I answered. "But it's like I always told you, the road to ruin is paved with crude inventions."

Nick rolled his eyes and grinned slightly as he got up and gathered the boxes he had dumped on the kitchen table. "Inventions!" he said, laughing. "You mean like the time you told me to use Mom's vacuum cleaner to rake the yard?"

"It would have worked if you hadn't hit the sprinkler," I said, scooping some raspberry jam out of the jar next to me.

Nick just shook his head and started hauling the boxes toward the stairs. "Or how about the time you told me to cut the sleeves off my shirt so Mom wouldn't see where I tore it? Or the time . . ." His voice trailed off in the distance as he headed up the stairs.

Sure, I remembered all those things. It was clear Nick had a great memory, too. It was also clear that it could take some time to put the last few days behind us. And believe me, that movie and Nick's "escape" were things I would just as soon forget.

One thing was sure, though: Nick and I would have a lot more memories—some good, some bad. If we were smart, we'd use all of them to make the road ahead a little easier to follow. Or at least a little clearer. Knowing Nick and me, that road would be paved with fun, friendship, and above all, adventure.

Stay tuned, sports fans. . . .